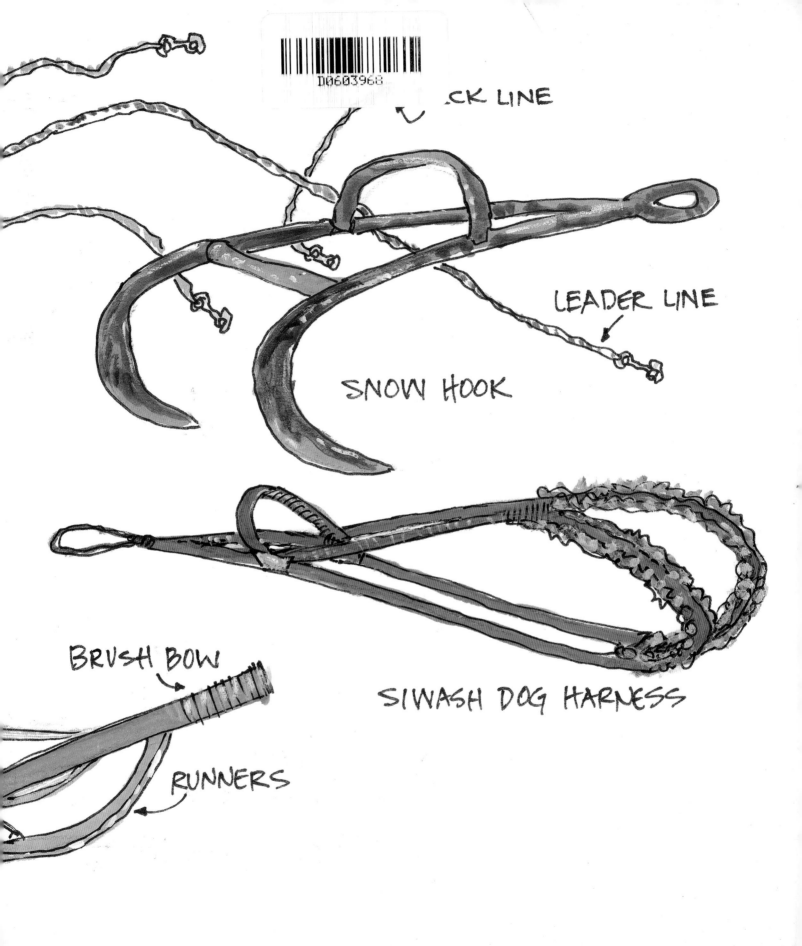

CK LINE

SNOW HOOK

LEADER LINE

BRUSH BOW

RUNNERS

SIWASH DOG HARNESS

SLED DOGS RUN

JONATHAN LONDON

Illustrations by JON VAN ZYLE

Walker & Company
New York

First published in the United States of America in 2005
by Walker Publishing Company, Inc.

Published simultaneously in Canada by Fitzhenry and Whiteside,
Markham, Ontario L3R 4T8

For information about permission to reproduce selections from this
book, write to Permissions, Walker & Company, 104 Fifth Avenue,
New York, New York 10011

Library of Congress Cataloging-in-Publication Data
available upon request
ISBN 0-8027-8957-9 (hardcover)
ISBN 0-8027-8958-7 (reinforced)

The artist used acrylic on Masonite panels to create the
illustrations for this book.

Book design by Maura Fadden Rosenthal/Mspaceny

Visit Walker & Company's Web site at www.walkeryoungreaders.com

Printed in Hong Kong

10 9 8 7 6 5 4 3 2 1

To Jon and Jona, for the love of it —J. L.

To all young people
who dream of running their
own sled dog team . . .
and to Logan,
who aspires to
other dreams —J. V. Z.

They were born in the spring:
fat, tumbling puppy balls
full of fresh puppy smell
and puppy life.

There was Skookum and Hawk and Bamboo.
Here in Alaska, in the Far North, *Skookum* means "smart."
"See how Hawk and Bamboo chase him but can't
catch him," says Papa. "He will be the leader."

Now, in summer, the training begins.
Sled dogs run. That's what they live for.
To run. To run and pull.

First, they wear a harness, to get used to it.
Then they pull a small log, bouncing and skidding behind them.

In the fall, they pull a cart for the first time.
Papa runs behind me. I call out:
"Skookum! Hawk! Bamboo! Good dogs!"
For now, they run with older dogs.
I can't wait till the first snow.

In the winter, the snow comes.
White on white, as soft as owl's feathers.
I lie down in the softness and make a snow angel,
but my dogs are eager to run.

And by February, they are ready to pull as a team—
with me as musher. My first solo run! Mama heats
up a sloppy stew. The dogs must eat fast before it freezes.

Mama gives me a hug. "You will love the quiet," she says, "and the oneness with nature." "You will love the speed," Papa says, "and the sense of freedom."

When I come with the harnesses,
the dogs go crazy.
They run in circles,
howling and crying and yipping with joy.

Hitched to the gang line,
they are raring to go.
Mama says, "Be back by dark!"
In the North, in the winter, dark comes early.
Papa says, "Trust the dogs.
They will know the way!"

I pull the snow hook and shout, "Hike!"
The sled feels like it's leaving the ground.
Whoosh! We're off—the dogs straining, tugging,
running out before me, huffing puffs of breath.

We are racing cloud shadows.
We are racing a snowy owl.
We are racing the wind.

We spook a snowshoe hare
and fly after it.
The sled whips.
The runners *shusshh*.
The collars and snaps jingle.
Hare disappears into white.

The dogs smell moose
and go after it.
Moose stops and turns around—
fire in her eyes.
With one kick, a moose can cave in a rib cage.
That's what Papa says.

I yell "Haw!" and my dogs swerve left,
away from the moose.
I yell "Gee!" and my dogs swerve right,
their keen noses scenting the trail.

I hear a howl.
Is it the howl of wolves?
The hair stands up on my dogs' necks.

No, it is the howling wind blowing the snow sideways.
I hang on to the sled handle for dear life.
The storm is a hungry wolf, eating up the light.
Just as we hit a frozen lake we are blinded.
We are lost.

But I remember what Papa says:
"Trust the dogs.
They will know the way!"
The dogs are my eyes.

Through the snow-blind world we drive.
All I hear is the howl of the wind—
and the boom of the lake ice shifting.
"Skookum! Hawk! Bamboo! Take me home!"

Suddenly the wind dies to a whisper,
and the air clears, like a clean window.
"Whoa!" I call. We come to a stop.
"Good dogs! Good team!"
The sun is down and the full moon is rising,
tipping its golden light.

When my dogs stop panting,
there's a silence
as quiet as owl's breath.

hen I see, beyond the long blue shadows of the spruce: lights. Our cabin in the woods!
Home.
And we become a part of the night and the moon and the snow and the trees and we run.

"Skookum! Hawk! Bamboo! Hike!"

We run to keep up with our hearts.

Author's Note

Dogs and humans have a relationship that spans almost fourteen thousand years. Our earliest ancestors started raising wolf pups, selectively breeding them until they evolved into the first domesticated dogs: our companions, guards, hunters, herders, and haulers. Sled dogs are haulers, natural-born pullers. For centuries, peoples of northern regions across Asia, Europe, and North America have depended on dog teams for winter travel. Now people from all over are rediscovering the rewards of raising and caring for sled dogs and running them for the sheer joy of it.

Siberian huskies—the sled dogs in this book—were developed over a period of three thousand years by the Chukchi and other tribal peoples of Siberia. The Chukchi relied on their sled dogs for survival in one of the coldest climates on Earth. According to Chukchi belief, two huskies guard the gates of heaven; they turn away anybody who has shown cruelty to a dog in his or her lifetime.

The bond between a dog and his driver, or "musher," begins when the dog is a puppy, and puppies need a lot of love and care. Though puppies naturally want to pull, they must be trained to pull as a team, responding to voice commands. A team of mature sled dogs is so powerful it can pull a six-thousand-pound truck out of a ditch.

Sled dogs love to run while pulling a sled behind them. The special bond that mushers feel for their dogs when they run verges on a kind of magic—a magic that takes place when the snow and the silence and the musher and the dogs are one.